Fun at the Fair

by Kate Egan
illustrated by Ken Edwards

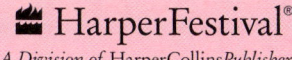

A Division of HarperCollins*Publishers*

The sun was just rising over Ponyville.
The ponies were getting an early start.
They were going to a fair!

"Let's have a race!" Minty squealed. The ponies ran through the meadow until they reached the fair.

The friends bounded through the gate.
The fair stretched as far as they could see.

There was so much to do!

"Let's go on the bumper cars!" cried Sunny Daze.
She shared a car with Butterscotch.
They crashed into Rainbow Dash!

"Anyone want to try the water slide?" asked Wysteria.
The ponies got soaked,
but they soon dried off in the warm sun.

Butterscotch wanted a picture of all her friends.
It would remind her of their day at the fair.
The ponies crowded into a photo booth.
They made funny faces for the camera!

Then Sunny Daze said, "Let's try some games." She leaped to a row of booths. The ponies were ready to play!

Minty went first.
She had to jump on a platform.
If she jumped hard enough, a bell would ring.

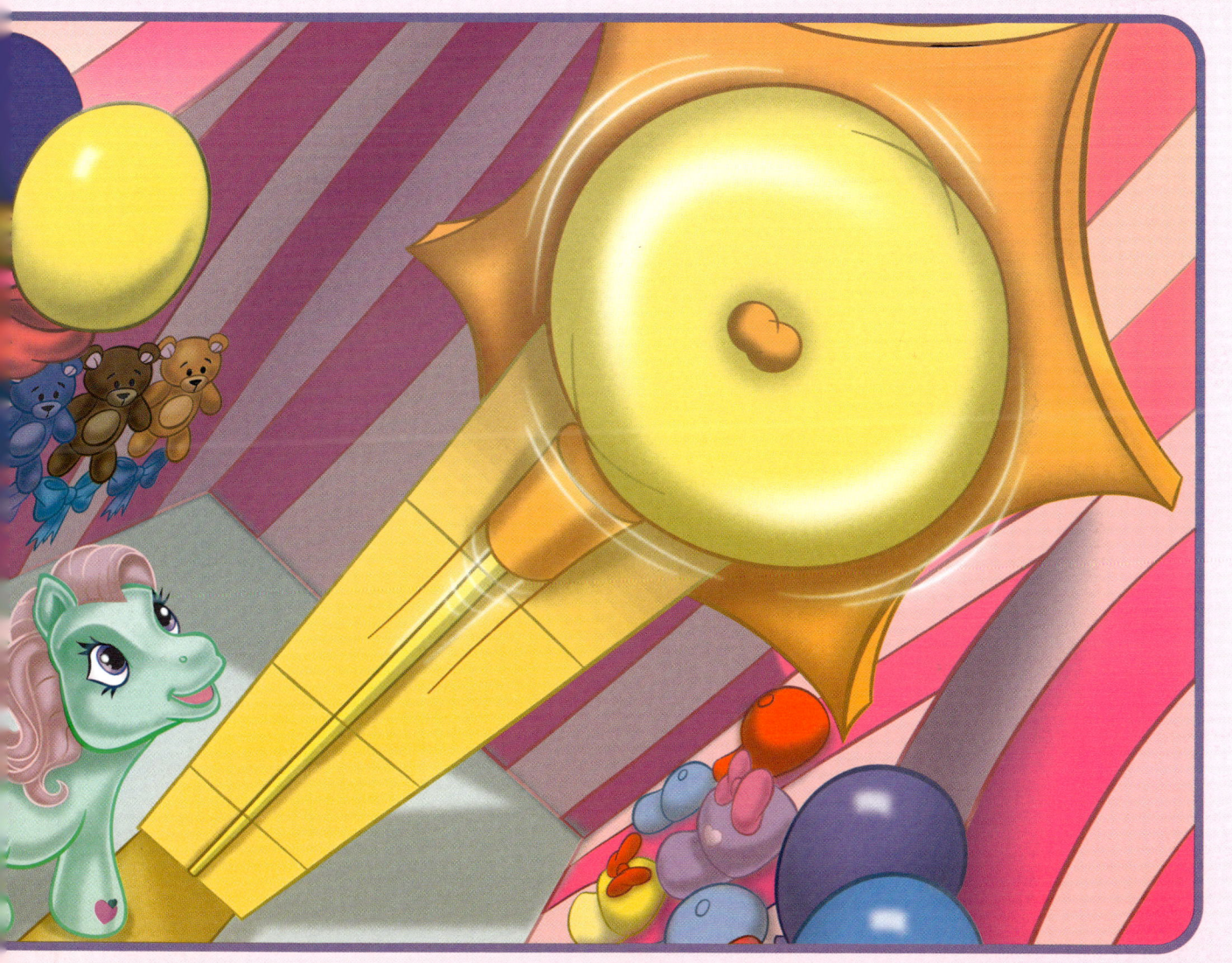

Minty jumped with all her might.
The bell rang—Minty won!
Her prize was a cute cap.

Minty's prize was stylish, but it was not what she wanted.
She had her eye on a teddy bear!
If Minty won at three booths in a row, she could trade in her prizes for the bear.

Minty's friends were still taking turns on the platform.
Minty headed for the next booth.
She thought of the bear. Then she tossed a water balloon.
This time she won a necklace!

Minty's friends cheered her on at the next booth.
"You can do it, Minty!" said Wysteria.
"Pony power!" shouted Sparkleworks.

The third game looked easy.
Minty just had to kick a ball through a goal.
But she didn't win with her first kick.
She didn't win with her second kick, either.

The other ponies decided to go on the Ferris wheel.
They waved to Minty from the top.
Minty was too busy to see them.

Minty missed a lot of fun.
Rainbow Dash went to the face-painting booth.
She had rainbows painted on both her cheeks.

Sunny Daze went on the roller coaster.

And Butterscotch found lots of stickers for her scrapbooks.

Minty kept on playing,
but the ball always went in the wrong direction.
Minty still wanted to win the bear,
but she was starting to feel discouraged.

Suddenly, Wysteria was beside her.
"I'll bet you're tired," she said.
"Maybe you just need a break."
The friends shared an ice-cream cone.
Then they returned to the game.

Now Minty was ready to try again.
She took a deep breath. Then she kicked the ball.
It went right into the goal.
Minty had won the third prize!

Minty traded her three prizes for the teddy bear.
She gave the bear a squeeze.
Then she gave Wysteria a squeeze, too.
A friend like Wysteria was the best prize of all!

And fireworks were the best end to the ponies' day at the fair.